For Anna — SG
For my parents — RB

Published by
PEACHTREE PUBLISHERS, LTD.
1700 Chattahoochee Avenue
Atlanta, Georgia 30318-2112

www.peachtree-online.com

First published in Great Britain in 2000 by Bloomsbury Publishing Plc
38 Soho Square, London WIV 5DF

Designed by Dawn Apperley

Printed and bound by South China Printing Co.

10 9 8 7 6 5 4 3 2

ISBN 1-56145-224-6

Cataloging-in-Publication Data is available from the Library of Congress

# Who Is It?

### Sally Grindley and Rosalind Beardshaw

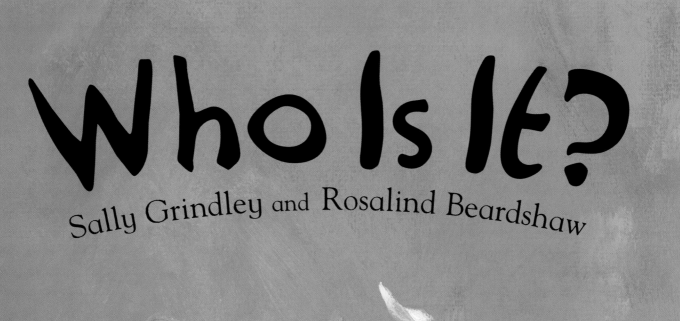

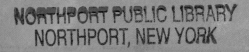

Someone's eating
Mr. Bear's porridge.

Someone's sitting in
Mrs. Bear's chair.

Someone's sleeping
in Baby Bear's bed.

Who is it?

It's Goldilocks!

Wake up, Goldilocks.
The Bears are
after you!

Someone's going into Grandma's cottage.

Someone's eating Grandma up.

Someone's wearing Grandma's nightclothes.

Who is it?

# It's the Wolf!
## Look out, Little Red Riding Hood!

Someone's built a wooden house under a bridge.

Someone hears
a trip-trapping
over his head.

Someone's feeling hungry
and he's ready to pounce!

Who is it?

It's the Troll!

Run away, Billy Goats Gruff!

Someone's climbing up
a great big beanstalk.

Someone's going
through a great big door.

Someone's stealing the giant's enormous bag of gold!

Who is it?

It's Jack.
And the Giant's waked up!
Get out of there fast, Jack!

Someone's watching you
read this book.

Someone can't wait till you
reach the last page.

Someone's ready with a **BIG** surprise for you.

Who is it?

It's me!

And I'm coming
to get you
NOW!